The
Horned
Toad
Prince

To my mom, the real Rhebajo, and her prince, Jack.

Thank you, Carmen Deedy, mi amiga.

—J. M. H.

For Kim.

—M. A.

Published by
PEACHTREE PUBLISHERS
1700 Chattahoochee Avenue
Atlanta, Georgia 30318-2112

www.peachtree-online.com

Text © 2000 by Jackie Mims Hopkins
Illustrations © 2000 by Michael Austin

First trade paperback edition published in 2010

Manufactured in March 2010 by Imago in Singapore

Book design by Michael Austin and Loraine M. Joyner
Composition by Melanie McMahon Ives

10 9 8 7 (hardcover)
10 9 8 7 6 5 4 3 2 1 (trade paperback)

Library of Congress Cataloging-in-Publication Data

Hopkins, Jackie.
    The horned toad prince / Jackie Hopkins ; illustrated by Michael Austin.--1st ed.
        1 v. (unpaged) : col. ill. ; 24 x 26 cm.
        Summary: In this retelling of "The Frog Prince," a spunky cowgirl loses her new sombrero and is helped by a horned toad on the understanding that she will do three small favors for him.
        ISBN 13: 978-1-56145-195-1 / ISBN 10: 1-56145-195-9 (hardcover)
        ISBN 13: 978-1-56145-548-5 / ISBN 10: 1-56145-548-2 (trade paperback)
        [1. Fairy tales. 2. Folklore.] I. Austin, Michael, ill. II. Title.

PZ8.H7785 Ho 2000
398.22--dc21
[E]   99-047896

The Horned Toad Prince

Jackie Mims Hopkins

Illustrated by

Michael Austin

PEACHTREE

ATLANTA

For: Fiona,

Jasso

Your dreams!

2015

Jackie Mims Hopkins

Reba Jo loved to twang her guitar and sing while the prairie wind whistled through the thirsty sagebrush.

Singing with the wind was one of the ways Reba Jo entertained herself on the lonesome prairie. Sometimes she amused herself by racing her horse, Flash, against a tumbleweed cartwheeling across her daddy's land.

But her favorite pastime of all was roping. She lassoed cacti, water buckets, fence posts, and any unlucky critter that crossed her path.

One blustery morning, as she was riding the range looking for something to lasso, Reba Jo came upon a dry riverbed. Her daddy had warned her to stay away from these *arroyos.* He'd told her that a prairie storm could blow in quicker than a rattlesnake's strike, causing a flash flood to rip through the riverbed. The swift water would wash away anything or anyone in its way.

Reba Jo knew she should turn back. But right at the edge of this gully she spied a vulture, all fat and sassy, sitting on top of a dried-up old well, just daring her to toss her spinning rope around his long ugly neck.

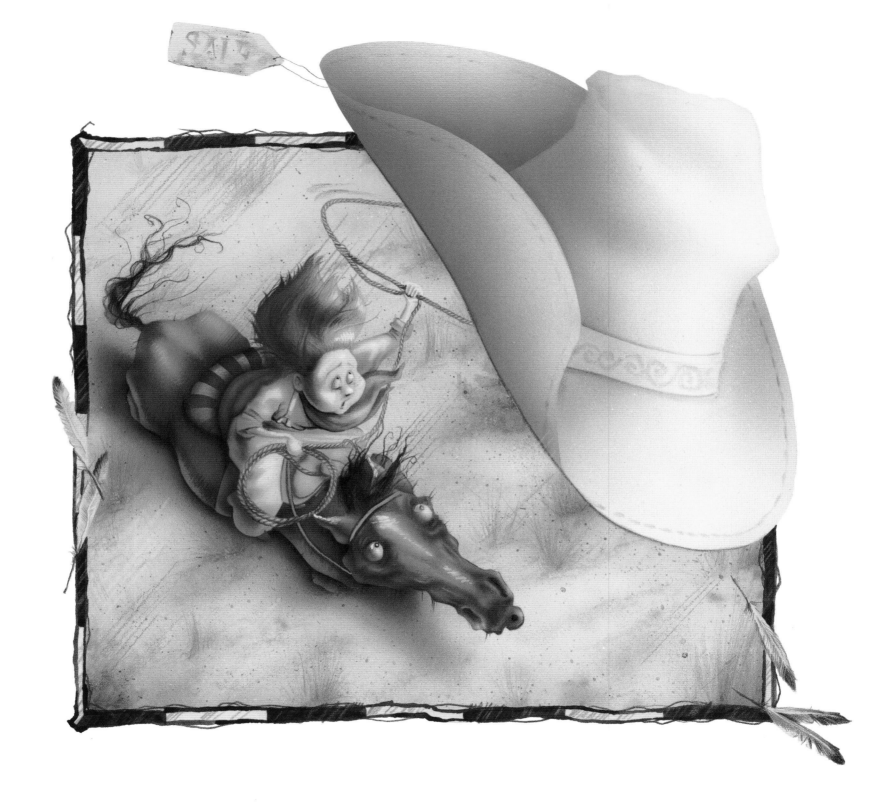

As Reba Jo's lasso whirled into the air, a great gust
of wind came whipping through the *arroyo* and
blew her new cowgirl hat right off her head and
down to the bottom of the dusty old well.

Reba Jo scrambled to the edge of the well. She peered down into the darkness and commenced to crying. Suddenly she heard a small voice say, *"¿Qué pasa, señorita?"*

She looked around and wondered if the wind blowing through the *arroyo* was fooling her ears.

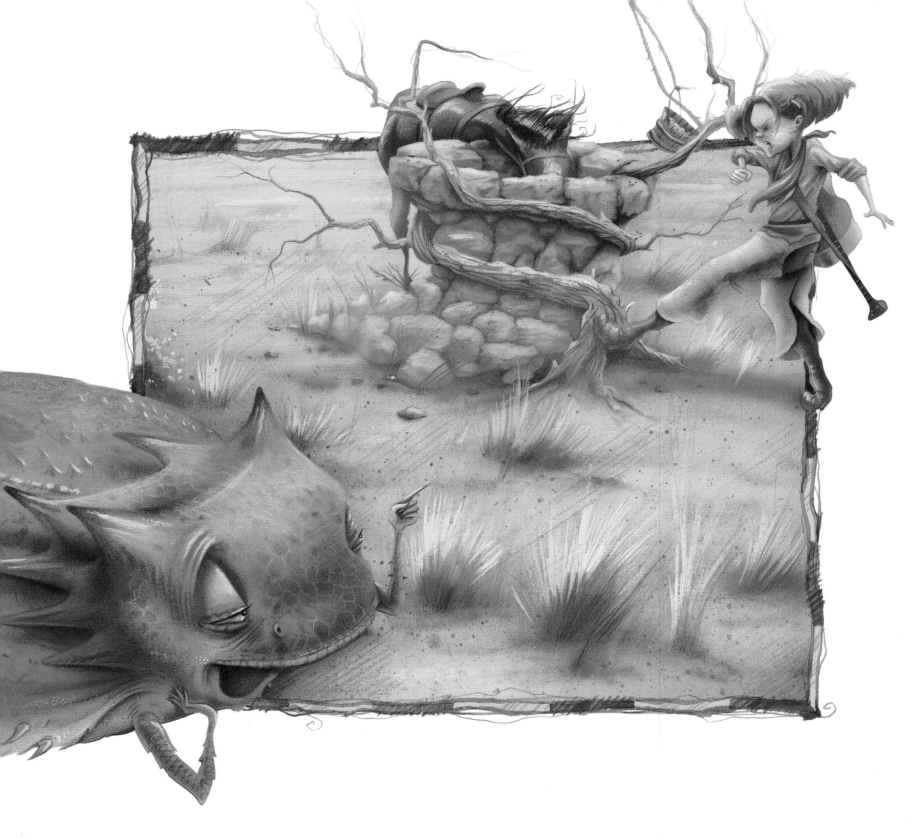

But then, there in the sand, she spotted
a big fat horned toad looking up at her.
"What's the matter, *señorita?*" he asked again.

"Oh," she cried, "the brand-new hat my daddy
bought for me just blew down into this stinkin' old well.
I'll never be able to get it out, and I'll be in a peck of trouble
when he finds out I've been playin' down here near the *arroyo.*"

The horned toad looked at her slyly and said, "I'll fetch your
sombrero for you if you will do *tres pequeños* favors for me."

She sniffed and asked, "Three small favors? Like what?"

"All you have to do is feed me some chili, play your *guitarra*
for me, and let me take a *siesta* in your *sombrero.*"

"Some chili, a song, and a nap in my hat? I don't think so,
amigo," replied Reba Jo.

"Okay, *señorita*, but do you mind if I follow you home and listen as you explain to your *padre* where your new *sombrero* is, and how it got there?"

"Good point, toad," Reba Jo said. "You've got yourself a deal."

Reba Jo placed the little critter in a splintered wooden bucket and carefully lowered him down the dry well, where he retrieved Reba Jo's hat.

Then, without so much as a *muchas gracias*, Reba Jo snatched her hat from the horned toad and galloped home. As she rode out of sight, she ignored the horned toad's cries of "*¡Espera!* Wait up, *señorita*, wait up!"

'**Long about midday,** when Reba Jo had sat down to eat, she heard a tap, tap, tapping at the ranch house door.

Reba Jo opened the door, but when she saw it was the fat horned toad, she slammed the door in his face.

His small voice called, *"Señorita, señorita, por favor.* Please let me come in."

The horned toad rapped on the door again. This time Reba Jo's father opened it and spotted the little fella on the porch.

"*Hola, señor,*" said the horned toad.

"Well howdy, mister toad. What brings you here?"

"A little deal that I made with your daughter, *señor.*"

"What's this all about, Reba Jo?" her father asked her.

Reba Jo admitted that the horned toad had done her a favor and in return she had promised to feed him some chili, play her guitar for him, and let him take a nap in her hat.

"Now, Reba Jo," said her daddy, "if you strike a bargain in these parts, a deal's a deal. Come on in, pardner, you look mighty hungry."

"I am indeed. *Tengo mucha hambre*," said the horned toad. "I hope that is chili I smell." He peeked at Reba Jo's meal.

"Dadburn it!" Reba Jo muttered. She pushed her bowl of chili toward him.

Soon the horned toad's belly was bulging. "Now, for a little *serenata*," he said.

Reba Jo stomped over, grabbed her guitar, and belted out a lullaby for her guest.

Then the drowsy little horned toad eyed Reba Jo's hat and yawned, saying, "That lovely music has made me *muy soñoliento*. I'm ready for my *siesta*."

"Forget it, Bucko," Reba Jo snapped. "You're not gettin' near my hat. No lizard cooties allowed!"

"Now, *señorita*, remember what your wise *padre* said about striking a bargain in these parts," said the clever little horned toad.

"I know, I know," grumbled Reba Jo, "a deal's a deal." And with that, she flipped him like a cow chip into her hat.

"Before I take my *siesta*, I have just one more favor to ask," said the horned toad.

"Now what?" asked Reba Jo.

"Would you give me a kiss, *por favor?*" asked the horned toad.

"You've gotta be kiddin'!" shrieked Reba Jo. "You know dang well a kiss wasn't part of this deal, you low-life reptile."

"If you do this one last thing for me, we'll call it even, and I'll be on my way *pronto*," the horned toad said.

"You'll leave right away?" Reba Jo asked suspiciously. "You promise?"

"*Sí, te lo prometo*," agreed the horned toad.

Reba Jo thought hard for a minute. She glared at the horned toad. "I can't believe I'm even considerin' this," she said, "but if it means you'll leave right now...pucker up, Lizard Lips."

Before Reba Jo could wipe the toad
spit off her lips, a fierce dust devil spun
into the yard, swept the horned toad
off his feet, and whirled him around
in a dizzying cloud of prairie dust.

When the dust cleared, there before Reba Jo stood a handsome young *caballero*.

"Who are you?" Reba Jo demanded, staring at the gentleman.

"I am Prince Maximillian José Diego López de España."

"Whoa, how did this happen?" Reba Jo asked in amazement.

"Many, many years ago when I came to this country, I offended the great spirit of the *arroyo*. The spirit put a spell on me and turned me into a horned toad. For many years I've been waiting for a cowgirl like you to break the spell. *Muchas gracias* for my freedom, *señorita*. Now I'll be leaving as I promised."

"Now hold on for just a dadburn minute," said Reba Jo, stepping in front of the nobleman.

"I recollect my daddy readin' me a story where somethin' like this happened. Aren't we supposed to get hitched and ride off into the sunset?"

With a twinkle in his eye, the *caballero* replied, "*Lo siento.* So sorry, Reba Jo, when you strike a bargain in these parts, a deal's a deal.

¡Adiós, señorita!"